The Magic Tree

A Folktale from Nigeria

by T. Obinkaram Echewa ❧ illustrated by E. B. Lewis

MORROW JUNIOR BOOKS ❧ NEW YORK

Note: The name Mbi is pronounced MMH-BEE.

Watercolors were used for the full-color illustrations.
The text type is 16-point Usherwood Medium.

Text copyright © 1999 by T. Obinkaram Echewa
Illustrations copyright © 1999 by E. B. Lewis

All rights reserved. No part of this book may be reproduced or
utilized in any form or by any means, electronic or mechanical,
including photocopying, recording, or by any information storage
and retrieval system, without permission in writing from the Publisher.

Published by Morrow Junior Books
a division of William Morrow and Company, Inc.
1350 Avenue of the Americas, New York, NY 10019
www.williammorrow.com

Printed in Hong Kong by South China Printing Company (1988) Ltd.

10 9 8 7 6 5 4 3 2 1

Library of Congress Cataloging-in-Publication Data
Echewa, T. Obinkaram.
The magic tree: a folktale from Nigeria/by T. Obinkaram Echewa;
illustrated by E. B. Lewis.
p. cm.
Summary: Mbi, an orphan boy, is constantly asked to "do this" and "do
that" by his many unkind relatives until a special tree grows, just for him.
ISBN 0-688-16231-2 (trade)—ISBN 0-688-16232-0 (library)
[1. Folklore—Nigeria.   2. Orphans—Folklore.]   I. Lewis, Earl B., ill.
II. Title.   PZ8.1.E17Mag 1999   398.2   [E]—DC20   91-19770   CIP AC

To my grandchildren
                  —T.O.E.

In memory of my father, Charles E. Lewis
                  —E.B.L.

Once there was an orphan boy named Mbi, who lived in a village with many unkind relatives. You would have thought his middle name was "Do this!" or "Do that!" because people were constantly saying to him, "Mbi, do this! Mbi, do that!" When it was time to eat or to play, no one thought of him. But whenever there was work to do, everyone called his name:

"Mbi, where are you?"

"Mbi, there is no water in my water pot. Go to the well and fetch a pot of water for me."

"Mbi, fetch me some wood for my fire."

"Mbi, I am going to the farm to hoe a ridge. You must go with me."

Beginning very early in the morning when the first person in the village woke up, it was "Mbi, wake up so you can do this! Mbi, sleepyhead, wake up and do that!"

All day long, as men and women worked on the farms or around their houses, they never stopped saying, "Where is Mbi? Mbi, hurry up and do this! Mbi, why didn't you do that? Mbi, as soon as you finish this, do that!"

Even late at night, long after the other children had finished playing their moonlight games and had gone to bed, grown-ups would come to Mbi where he sat sleepily in whatever corner he could find and say, "Mbi, wake up and do this! Mbi, stop dozing and do that!"

But when it was time to eat, no one could remember Mbi's name. While each family sat together in a circle for dinner, Mbi sat by himself at a distance, wearing his raggedy clothes and playing a silly game to distract himself. Sometimes his mouth and his throat would move up and down as he watched other children chew and swallow their food. Sometimes hunger made his stomach growl.

When the other people had finished eating, Mbi would run to their plates to see if he could find any scraps. He would lick the bowls and chew the bones the other children had left behind.

Then he would hear, "Mbi, hurry up and wash the dinner dishes!"

When the other children played, they never included Mbi in their games, unless a team was short one person or they wanted to put him in the middle of their play circle and make fun of him.

One day, while everyone else was eating dinner, Mbi thought that maybe if he did not watch other people as they ate, he would not feel so hungry. He decided to go and sit under the *udara* tree, which grew a short distance from the compound. This was not the season for *udara,* but as Mbi was sitting under the tree, all of a sudden a large ripe fruit fell from it, *pom*!

Mbi reached for the fruit—the largest and roundest *udara* fruit he had ever seen. It smelled so delicious that Mbi became breathless in his eagerness to squeeze it open. And when it touched his lips, it made not just his mouth but even his ears tingle with delight. He tilted back his head, closed his eyes, and sucked at it with relish. This was the most scrumptious fruit he had ever tasted.

Very soon all that was left of the big *udara* fruit were four brown seeds. Mbi took the largest seed and, after making a hole in the ground with a stick, planted the seed and covered it with earth.

As Mbi watched the place where he had planted the seed, he was surprised to see a small shoot come out. Already? he thought. Wow!

"It is yours," he heard a voice say.

"What?" Mbi said, surprised and a bit frightened. He looked around but saw no one.

"It is yours," the voice said again. "Sing to it. Ask it to grow."

All of a sudden a song came to Mbi's mind, and he began singing:

"Udaram to-o-oh! (My *udara* tree, grow!)
Nda!
To-o-oh! To-o-oh! To-o-oh! (Grow! Grow! Grow!)
Nda!"

As Mbi was singing, the tiny shoot began to grow.
Very soon it was the size of a shrub. Soon after that
it became the size of a bush, then a tree, then a
very big, full-grown *udara* tree, with many, many
branches and lots and lots of green leaves.

When the tree was full grown, Mbi heard the voice say, "Ask it to make fruit."

Mbi began singing:

"Udaram mia! (My udara tree, make fruit!)
Nda!
Mia! Mia! Mia! (Make fruit! Make fruit! Make fruit!)
Nda!"

While Mbi was singing, flowers appeared on the tree. Soon there were little green *udara* fruit everywhere among the leaves. Right before Mbi's eyes, the fruit became bigger and bigger and soon were full grown.

The branches of the *udara* tree began to sag and hang down from the weight of the fruit. Soon the fruit began to ripen and turn yellow, and then, almost immediately afterward, the fruit were fully ripe and sweet smelling.

Mbi stood with his head tilted back and his eyes wide open. He wished he could sample the fruit. No sooner was the wish on his mind than a fruit dropped from the tree right into his hands! When he tasted this *udara* fruit, it was so delicious that he pursed his lips, closed his eyes, shook his head, and stomped his feet!

I wish I could pluck some of the fruit without climbing the tree or using a long stick, Mbi thought. As soon as the thought was on his mind, one of the branches of the tree began bending down, lower and lower, until Mbi could reach it with his hands. After Mbi had plucked a handful of delicious fruit, the branch went back to its original place.

Mbi then sat down and ate all the *udara* fruit his heart could desire and his belly could hold. Next he decided to play games with his tree.

"That branch over there," he said, pointing, "bend down, so I can pluck a fruit!"

Done!

"A little lower," Mbi said, "so I don't have to stand on my tiptoes!"

Done!

"Branch over there," Mbi said, "drop one fruit for me!"

Done!

"Branch over there, I want two—no, four—no, ten of the most delicious *udara* fruit you have!"

Done!

Mbi was having so much fun with his tree that he did not hear a chorus of loud and impatient voices asking for him:

"Mbi, where are you?" the first voice asked angrily. "I thought I asked you to fetch me a pot of water from the well."

"Foolish boy, are you being idle again?" another voice said. "You were supposed to go to the bush and gather firewood for me. How am I supposed to cook breakfast for my children tomorrow morning without wood for a fire?"

"Not just foolish but also lazy," a third voice added. "Pots and bowls from this morning's breakfast are still unwashed. And now there are the bowls from this evening's supper."

All the people were surprised when they saw Mbi standing beside a big full-grown *udara* tree, full of fruit, when it wasn't even the season for *udara*.

"It is my *udara* tree," Mbi replied, when they asked him how the strange tree got there and what he was doing beside it.

"How is it your tree?"

"Who planted it?"

"How did it become full grown already?"

"And bear fruit?"

"And the fruit ripen?"

"In less than one day?"

Everyone was asking Mbi questions, one on top of the other. Soon the whole compound—men, women, and children—came to see the strange tree. Not long afterward all of the villagers were there, their hands on their hips, their heads tilted back, and their eyes wide with surprise as they looked at it.

With so many yellow, round, and sweet-smelling fruit on the *udara* tree, it was not long before sticks began flying as the bigger boys tried to knock down fruit. Some of the villagers used long sticks with hooks at their ends to try to pull down the fruit. A few boys even began climbing the tree. However, no matter what anybody did, no one could get even a single fruit from Mbi's tree.

Then Mbi began singing. To the amazement of everyone, as soon as the tree heard his words, fruit began falling. Soon the branches began bending down, so that people could reach up to them and pluck the fruit with their hands. That evening the whole village had an *udara* feast underneath Mbi's tree. They all ate as much *udara* as they wanted, and people even forgot to call Mbi to do this or do that for them.

The following day things were back to the way they used to be. It was again "Mbi, do this!" and "Mbi, do that!" from very early in the morning. That day one of the men took Mbi to help him chop down some trees. All day long they hacked at the big trees with axes: Chop! Chop! Chop! Hack! Hack! Hack! It was evening before the man and Mbi finally chopped down the last tree and were able to come home.

While the man went to eat dinner with his family, Mbi was left by himself as usual, tired, hungry, and thirsty, except that this time he could go and sit under his *udara* tree and eat as many fruit as he wanted.

When Mbi reached the tree, however, he found a boy—the meanest boy in the whole village—on top of the tree, trying to steal some of the fruit.

Mbi became angry and began singing to the tree:

"Udaram to-o-oh! (My *udara* tree, grow!)
Nda!
To-o-oh! To-o-oh! To-o-oh! (Grow! Grow! Grow!)
Nda!"

The tree began growing taller and taller. Taller and still taller!

"Stop it! Stop it!" the boy cried. "I am going to get you when I come down from here! Make it stop!"

The tree did not stop growing but instead continued to shoot into the sky. Very soon its branches were lost in the clouds, and with them the boy who had climbed the tree.

Mothers, fathers, and children rushed out from everywhere to see what was going on. People who were eating supper left their suppers half-eaten. Children who were playing left their games without finishing. First the whole compound and then the whole village came out.

The boy's mother began crying, "Oh, my son! Oh, my son! He is lost in the clouds! He is going to die. Someone, please help! Mbi, please make the tree come down! Only you can do it! Please! Please, Mbi! I will never again be unkind to you!"

Very soon all the villagers were begging Mbi to make the tree come down with the boy. "Mbi, please! Please, Mbi!" Their voices were gentle and full of sorrow, those same voices that used to say harshly, "Mbi, do this! Mbi, do that!"

The boy's mother ran to her kitchen, brought the best part of what she had made for supper, and served it to Mbi.

The boy's father took Mbi by the hand, hugged him, picked him up, carried him on his shoulders, and filled both of his hands with money.

The rest of the villagers gave Mbi many other gifts, called him endearing names, and pasted gift coins on his forehead.

Everyone promised to be kind to Mbi from that day on. Everyone promised to invite him to a meal if he would make the tree come down. Everyone promised not to ask him to do this or to do that if he would make the tree come down. All the children promised to include him in their games if he would make the tree come down. The adults promised to collect money and buy him new clothes.

More than that, they would hold a feast in his honor the very next day! To convince Mbi they meant what they said, they ran to their houses and right away gave him some of the things that they promised.

Standing in his new clothes, wearing a gold chain
around his neck, and surrounded by a pile of gifts,
Mbi began singing:

"*Udaram lowah!* (My *udara* tree, come down!)
Nda!
Lowah! Lowah! Lowah! (Come down! Come down!
    Come down!)
Nda!"

The tree began to come down. Lower and lower
it came. Soon the boy who had climbed it became
visible. All the villagers applauded when they first
saw him, and everyone began rejoicing. Finally the
tree came all the way down and the boy was able to
jump off, into the arms of his father.

Everyone cheered. "Thank you, Mbi!" they all said.
"Mbi, thank you!"

From that day onward everyone was kind to Mbi.

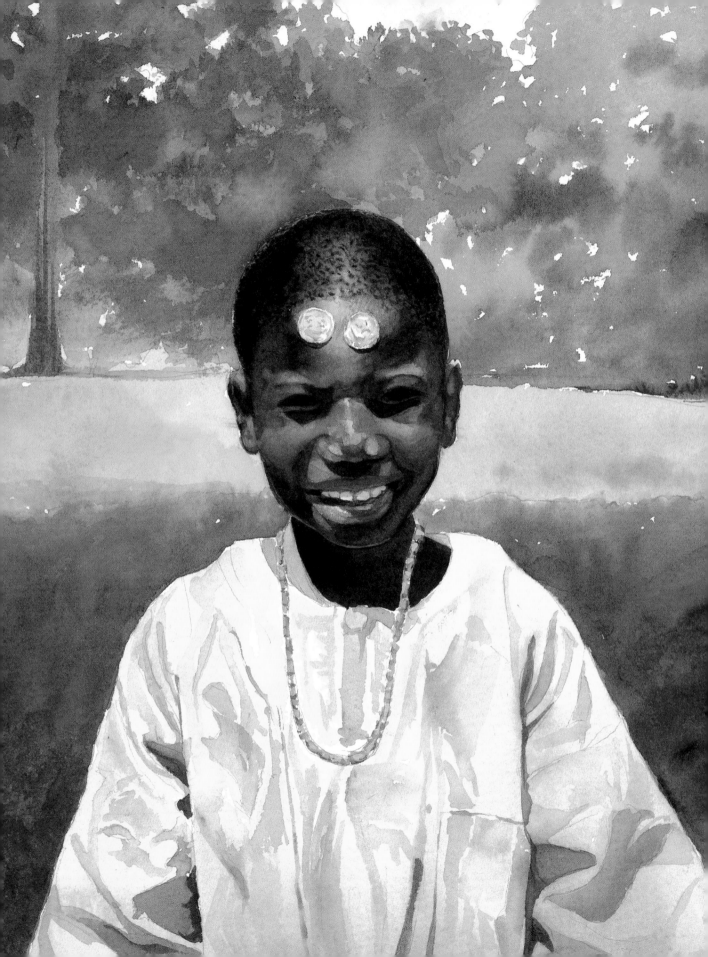